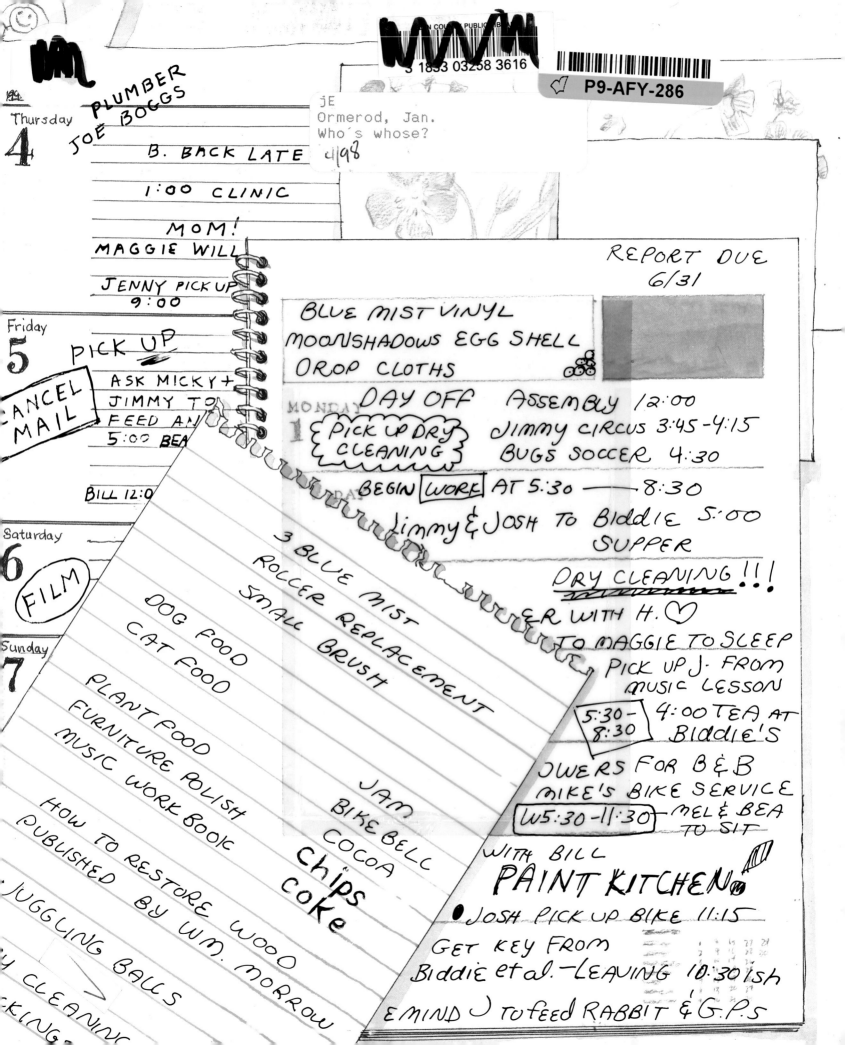

for
Frances

Pen and colored inks were used for the full-color illustrations. The text type is Avant Garde.

Published by Lothrop, Lee & Shepard Books
an imprint of Morrow Junior Books
a division of William Morrow and Company, Inc.
1350 Avenue of the Americas, New York, NY 10019
www.williammorrow.com

Printed in Singapore at Tien Wah Press.

1 2 3 4 5 6 7 8 9 10

Library of Congress Cataloging-in-Publication Data
Ormerod, Jan.
Who's whose?/ by Jan Ormerod [author and illustrator].
p. cm.
Summary: Three very busy families engage in such activities as school, soccer, piano playing, and cooking.
ISBN 0-688-14678-3 (trade)—ISBN 0-688-14679-1 (library)
[1. Family life—Fiction.]   I. Title.
PZ7.0634Wh 1997 [E]—DC20 96-27998 CIP AC

Who's Whose?

Jan Ormerod

Lothrop, Lee & Shepard Books · Morrow
New York

If the cat eats breakfast here,

lunch here,

and supper here . . .

who does it belong to?

On **Monday,** Josh rides his bike to school,

Maggie drives Molly and Bugs in the car,

and Mel and Bea walk, keeping an eye on Micky and Jimmy.

When Micky is sick at school,
Biddie and Boo Boo come to take him home.

Jenny and Bill come to school to hear Mel, Bea, and Josh sing.
Maggie invites Granny Bea for lunch next Sunday.

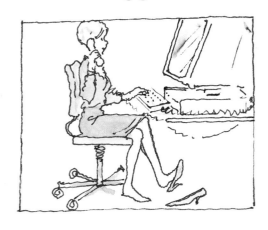

Who's
whose?

After school, Jenny picks up Jimmy
and takes him to circus class,

mails some letters,
pays some bills,
collects her dry cleaning,
buys a book for Micky
and some apples for Biddie,

and then comes back to collect Bugs after soccer.

Mel and Bea take Molly to the dentist,
then do homework while Josh watches TV.

So who forgot to take Jock for a walk?

On **Tuesday,** Bugs plays with Molly,

Maggie kisses Bugs better,

Micky plays with Jock,
and Jimmy practices piano while Josh watches TV.

Then Maggie drives Bill to the store
while Molly, Bugs, and Boo Boo
take care of the rabbit and guinea pigs, · · ·

and Biddie helps Bea and Mel with their homework
while she cooks supper.

Who grates the cheese?

Who sets the table?

Who helps carry in the groceries?

Who has homework?

Who watched TV?

Whose turn is it to wash up?
Who belongs where?

On **Wednesday** night when Jenny goes out,

whose shoes does she borrow?

Whose skirt does she wear?

Who paints her nails?

Who puts on her makeup?

And who gets most excited?

On **Thursday,** Granny Bea comes to visit
with a hat she has knitted for Boo Boo.
Molly sits on her knee, Jimmy juggles yarn balls for her,
Bugs does her a drawing, and Mel and Bea bake a cake.

Micky eats three pieces, and Maggie drives her home.
Who loves Granny Bea the most?

On **Fridays**, when Jenny works late,

JOSH —
TOP SHELF
350° FOR
20 MINUTES
CALL BIDDIE IF
ANY PROBLEMS
XOXO MOM

Jimmy sometimes sleeps here . . .

and sometimes sleeps here.

Tonight Josh is in charge, and
Mel and Bea are helping out.

Who is looking after whom?
And who ate Jock's supper?

When Mel, Micky, and Molly go to their dad's for the weekend,

Maggie may go for a walk with Biddie, Bill, Bugs, and Boo Boo
while Bea phones Mel;

or with Jenny, Jimmy, and Jock
while Josh watches TV.

Who gets the muddiest?

Some weekends, Bill keeps an eye on everyone

while Maggie, Biddie, and Jenny do yard work.

This **Saturday,** Bill takes Bugs, Boo Boo, Micky, Molly, Jimmy, and Jock to the park while Biddie has a rest on the sofa,

Mel and Bea do homework, and Josh watches TV.

Maggie helps Jenny paint her kitchen.

Who is most tired at the end of the day?

When
Jock
gets
into
trouble,

Maggie loses her temper and shouts,
Jenny loses her temper and cries,
Bugs and Molly get the giggles,
Micky and Jimmy get cross,
Boo Boo screams,
and Mel and Bea come running.

Josh makes everyone a cup of cocoa and cleans up.

Who is a good boy then?

On **Sunday,** Biddie, Bill, Bea, Bugs, and Boo Boo go away on vacation.

Who has lunch with Granny Bea?
Who waters the plants?

Who plays with the rabbit? Who cleans the guinea pig cage?

Who misses whom the most?

DEAR ALL —
    WE MISS YOU!
WISH YOU WERE
HERE. THE BEACH
IS GREAT!
LOTS OF LOVE—
    Biddle   ✗
    BILL   ✗
    BEA   ✗
    BUGS   ✗
    BOO BOO   ✗
(and BEAR) ✗

MAGGIE, MEL, MICKY,
MOLLY, JENNY, JOSH,
JIMMY, JOCK + CAT
c/o MRS. BLUE
19 THE AVENUE
BROOKLANDS

Who is pleased to
see them back
at the end of the week?

And who *does* that cat belong to anyway?

Monday
15

9:30 PLAYGROUP   * BOOTS! BUGS

MOM TO SIT, STAY OVER
DINNER JENNY + H — 7:30

Monday dinner Jenny's 7:30 —
15   meet H!
Mel + Bea baby-sitting   * chocs

day   10:30 Coffee Jenny
       2:00 bank Manager
       3:45 Molly + Bugs to park

day

6:00-8:00 computer class

to father's 6:30

Biddie + Bill to c

TOSFAX
Oregon

145

mom—
I'm sorry I
was grumpy!
Love,
mel